Ava's Homemade Hanukkah

Geraldine Woberg

illustrated by
Julia Seal

Albert Whitman & Company
Chicago, Illinois

It's Hanukkah—and Ava couldn't be more excited to celebrate! She loves eating latkes and playing dreidel, but the best part is when her relatives come over. It's a family tradition for everyone to bring their own unique Hanukkah menorahs—and their own stories.

The menorahs remind Ava of the ancient story of Hanukkah. "Have I ever told you about the brave Maccabees and the oil that lasted eight nights when it should only have been enough for one?" Ava asks her pet rabbit. "That's where your name comes from, Maccabee!"

Ava counts the Hanukkah menorahs on the table.
"See, Maccabee?" she asks. "If only we had one more,
there would be one for each night of Hanukkah."

As Ava ponders the problem, she hears a rustling sound on the floor.

"That's it!" she says. "I'll make a Hanukkah menorah of my own!"

Ava takes another glance at all the Hanukkah menorahs lined up on the table. "What kind of menorah would tell my story?" she asks Maccabee. "Let's take a closer look at these to get some ideas."

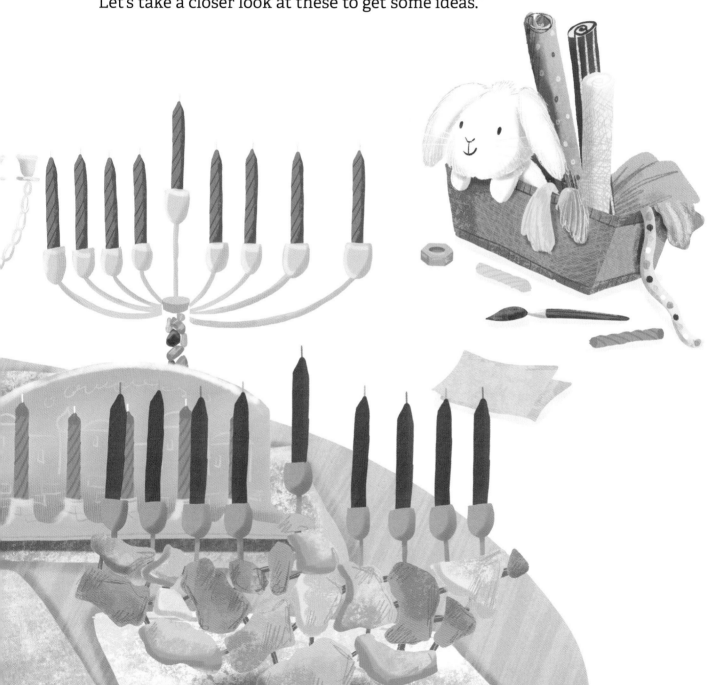

First, Ava and Maccabee look at Ava's mom's tin Hanukkah menorah. Light from the setting sun streams in through the window and reflects off the metal, causing it to sparkle.

Ava's mom explains. "This was the menorah the army gave me during my first Hanukkah away from home. When I saw the sunlight on the metal, I realized it was the same sun that was shining on my family, and I felt less homesick."

"Hear that, Maccabee?" Ava asks. "A Hanukkah menorah can help people feel connected to places they miss."

Next, they look at Pop-Pop's Hanukkah menorah. Instead of candles, it has corks that float in jars of oil.

Pop-Pop says, "When I was a kid, our Hanukkah menorah was a lot different than the ones my friends had. At first I hated being different, but later I realized how much I loved that my parents came from a place with its own traditions. And I stopped feeling like I had to be exactly the same as my friends."

"Hear that, Maccabee? Hanukkah menorahs don't all have to be the same." Ava pauses. "I'll have to make sure my Hanukkah menorah is unique!"

Next, they look at Aunt Rachel's Hanukkah menorah.
Inside are tiny shards of the glass Aunt Rachel and Aunt
Tamar broke as part of their wedding ceremony.

Aunt Rachel says, "Every time I see this Hanukkah menorah, I think of our beautiful wedding."

"With you as the world's most efficient flower girl!" adds Aunt Tamar as she nudges Ava and grins.

"Hear that, Maccabee? A Hanukkah menorah can help you remember a special event from your life." Ava remembers how much fun she had as the world's most efficient flower girl, dumping out all the flowers at once at the start of the aisle. Being in a wedding was a special event in Ava's life too.

Next to Aunt Rachel's Hanukkah menorah is Aunt Tamar's. The metal branches stand tall and proud, just like the tree Ava most loves to climb.

Aunt Tamar didn't grow up Jewish. But when her grandfather found the Hanukkah menorah in a box from *his* grandfather, she learned she had Jewish ancestors.

Aunt Tamar says, "I thought I only became part of a Jewish family after getting married. But now, every time I see this Hanukkah menorah, I love remembering that my family might have been Jewish even longer than I realized."

"Hear that, Maccabee?" Ava asks. "A Hanukkah menorah can help us feel proud of where we came from."

Ava looks out the window at her favorite tree. The roots reach deep into the earth, and the branches stretch in all directions.

Next, Ava and Maccabee check out Great-Aunt Sylvia's Hanukkah menorah, which was made long ago by a silversmith in Poland. Great-Aunt Sylvia thought the Hanukkah menorah had been lost when she and her family came to America seventy years ago. But just last year she learned that a childhood friend had been keeping it safe for her in Canada.

"It was wonderful to get my Hanukkah menorah back," says
Great-Aunt Sylvia. "But seeing my friend again was even better."

"Hear that, Maccabee?" Ava asks. "Someday you'll get to meet my friend Laura, who moved away last summer. Until then, my Hanukkah menorah can help us remember her."

After that, they look at Cousin Mike's Hanukkah menorah. The candle holders are shaped like the bears Mike works to protect in the forests of Montana.

Cousin Mike says, "When I light my Hanukkah menorah, I think about how I've loved animals ever since I was a kid. And now I get to help protect them! When I see you with your rabbit, it reminds me a little bit of myself when I was your age."

"Hear that, Maccabee?" Ava asks. "Maybe someday I'll have a job helping animals too."

Ava pauses. "A Hanukkah menorah can connect us to something we care about."

Finally, they look at the Hanukkah menorah belonging to Gabe, Ava's brother. Gabe made it himself, using small pieces of ancient pottery he brought back from his trip to Israel.

"Lighting my Hanukkah menorah makes me think about ancient Jerusalem. Our history goes back a long, long way," says Gabe.

"Hear that, Maccabee? A Hanukkah menorah connects people from today to ancient Jewish history." Ava pauses. "What's something ancient that can be part of my Hanukkah menorah?"

Ava can smell latkes frying in the kitchen: it's almost time to light the Hanukkah menorahs.

As quickly as she can, Ava gathers the supplies to make her own menorah.

- A floor tile from the first apartment they lived in, where Ava first learned to crawl.
- Metal nuts to hold candles in place, arranged in a shape no one has seen before.
- Some green wire from the flowers Ava wore in her hair when she was a flower girl at her aunts' wedding.
- A small twig that fell from her special tree.
- A friendship pin from Laura, her faraway friend.
- A toy rabbit that looks like Maccabee.

Ava looks at her Hanukkah menorah. Each piece helps to tell her own story and also connects to her family's stories. But something is still missing. How can she connect her Hanukkah menorah to ancient history, like Gabe did?

When Ava finishes an art project, the last step is usually to sign her name. But her Hanukkah menorah is not just any art project.

Using her best marker, Ava carefully writes the letters of her Hebrew name on the bottom corner of the tile. Now her Hanukkah menorah has something ancient on it too: Ava's Hebrew name.

Ava's whole family gathers around the table to admire her
Hanukkah menorah.

"Is that from our first apartment?" asks Gabe.

"Is that from our wedding?" asks Aunt Rachel.

Ava beams as she shows off the different parts of her
Hanukkah menorah.

Together, they sing the blessings and light all eight Hanukkah
menorahs—one for each night of the holiday.

"Did you hear that, Maccabee?" Ava asks. "Hanukkah menorahs can't talk, but they can help tell our stories."
"Rabbits help too!" she added.

For everyone who ever wondered
if they have a story to tell—GW

For Joseph and Amalie—JS

Library of Congress Cataloging-in-Publication data is on file with the publisher.
Copyright © 2022 by Albert Whitman & Company
Text by Geraldine Woberg
Illustrations by Julia Seal
First published in the United States of America in 2022
by Albert Whitman & Company
ISBN 978-0-8075-0495-6 (hardcover)
ISBN 978-0-8075-0496-3 (ebook)
Printed in China
10 9 8 7 6 5 4 3 2 1 WKT 26 25 24 23 22

Design by Theresa Venezia

For more information about Albert Whitman & Company,
visit our website at www.albertwhitman.com.